WATER FOR AFRICA

Bringing Hope and Love to a Thirsty Nation

To all of the water carriers – both physical and spiritual, God bless you!

- Natalie

First published in softcover by Dynamo Publishers in 2017

ISBN-13: 978-0-9954495-3-4

Copyright © 2017 by Natalie McNee

Cover design by Mary K. Biswas

Visit our website at www.dynamopublishers.com

National Library of Australia Cataloguing-in-Publication entry
Title: Water for Africa: Bringing Hope and Love to a Thirsty Nation
Written by Natalie McNee
Illustrated by Mary K. Biswas.
Notes: Includes bibliographical references.
Target Audience: For primary school age.
Subjects: Children's stories
Tanzania--Juvenile fiction
Tanzania--Social conditions--Juvenile fiction
Other Creators/Contributors: Biswas, Mary K., illustrator.

WATER FOR AFRICA

Bringing Hope and Love to a Thirsty Nation

Written by
Natalie McNee

Illustrated by
Mary K. Biswas

Dynamo Publishers

As the burning sun rose higher, Ashanti plodded to the water hole, carrying an empty bucket. Her little sister was asleep, tied to her back. Ashanti had been walking for a long time because it was a long way from her village to the water hole.

She looked down at her worn, mismatched shoes. They were her father's, and much too big. Her father let her wear them to protect her feet from thorns, but the shoes rubbed blisters on her heels and sides.

Ashanti kept careful watch all around. Walking to the water hole could sometimes be dangerous; there might be lions or hyenas nearby, as they came to drink the same water. Also, people from other villages came to the hole for water. They didn't like to share and if they saw Ashanti, they might chase her away with a stick.

When she reached the hole at last, Ashanti used a pan to scoop water into her bucket. Then she carefully balanced the bucket on her head. It was very heavy. Ashanti tried to walk carefully, tall and straight in her father's worn shoes. She did not want to spill a single drop of precious water.

When Ashanti's little sister awoke, Ashanti sang a song to keep her happy. Ashanti carried her sister and the water bucket for a long way back to the village. Her back and neck ached.

Ashanti's big sister used to carry the water bucket, but then she got sick from drinking dirty water. Now Ashanti had to fetch the water, sometimes going to the water hole two or three times a day.

I want to grow up and be a doctor, Ashanti thought as she stumbled along. But if I have to carry water, I can't go to school.

And if I can't go to school and learn to read and write, I will never be a doctor. Her heart felt as heavy as the water bucket. She struggled along, sweating in the hot sun.

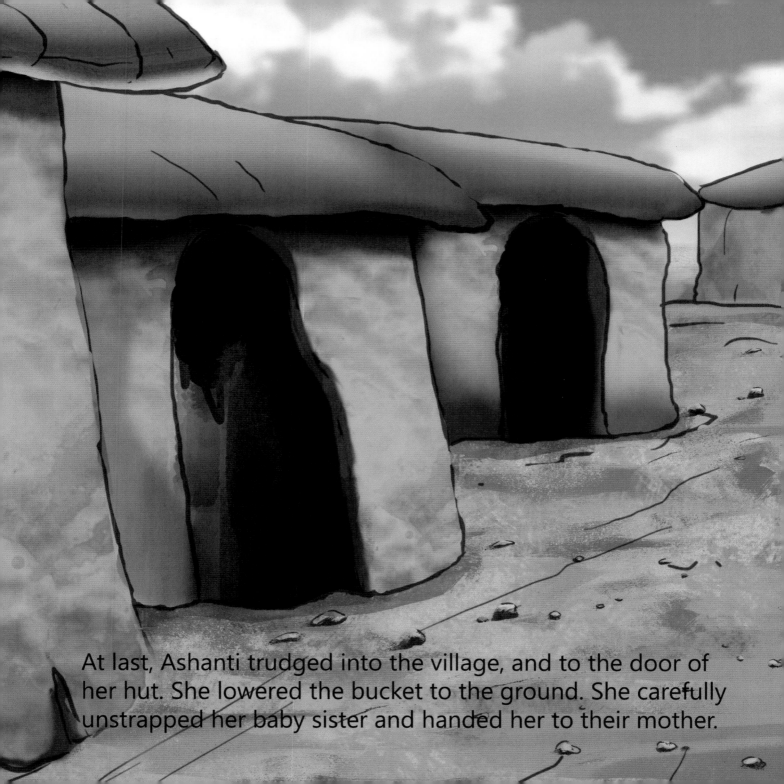

At last, Ashanti trudged into the village, and to the door of her hut. She lowered the bucket to the ground. She carefully unstrapped her baby sister and handed her to their mother.

Suddenly, village children ran past the hut, shrieking with excitement. "The water man is coming!" they shouted. "The water man will be here soon!" Ashanti could not believe her ears. Do wishes really come true? she wondered.

If the water man came, he would drill a well in the village. Then Ashanti would not have to walk so far, hot and tired and thirsty, with sore feet. She could go to school at last and learn many wonderful things.

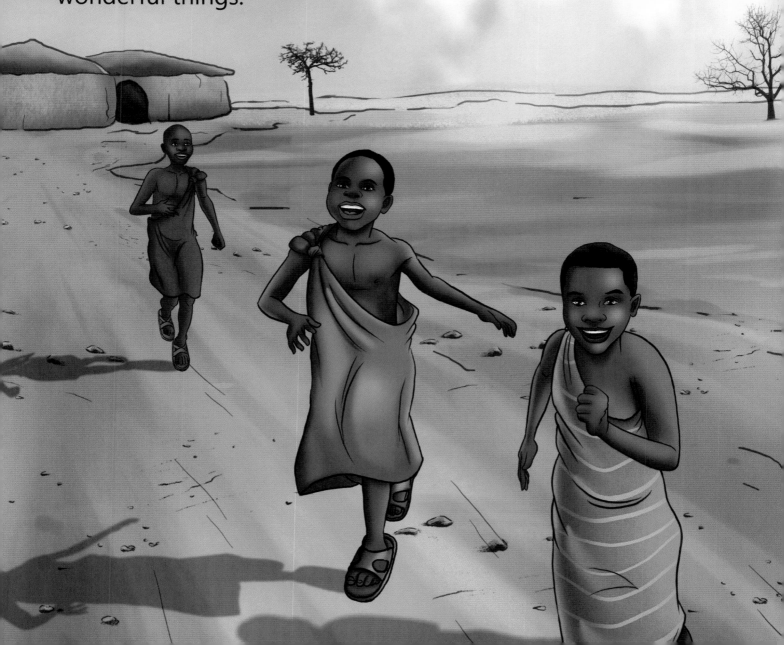

Ashanti kicked off those old shoes and ran after the children. They waited on the edge of the village.

The sun rose even higher. Ashanti squinted into the distance, wiping sweat from her face. She didn't see anything. Maybe the children were wrong. Her heart began to sink. I will have to carry water all my life, she thought.

"Look! The water man!" cried a girl.
A white truck slowly appeared over the hill. Ashanti's father and the other village men gathered around it as a white man stepped out. He shook their hands, and they talked together. Then the men started to haul machinery off the truck.

Ashanti's father looked over at her and gave her a big grin and a wave. Ashanti hugged herself in excitement. Her heart was turning cartwheels.

"The water man has really come," she whispered. "Now, will he bring water to us?"

The sun was slowly turning pink and red when her mamma called her into the hut. She had stayed all that time, watching the men drill down into the ground. They did not find any water that day. Ashanti was worried. Maybe wishes don't come true after all, she thought.

The next morning, Ashanti made the long trek to the water hole. Some mammas were washing their clothes in it already.

When Ashanti arrived back at her village, the men were at work again, drilling for water. There was a lot of noise and dust. Ashanti wished she could stay and watch, but she had to go back for more water as today was her own mamma's washing day, too.

As Ashanti was nearing the village with the second bucket of water balanced carefully on her head, she heard the shrill cries of the women. Cheering and whistling filled the air. What were the women cheering about?

Was there water at last? Was her wish coming true? Ashanti could not wait to find out. She set down her bucket and began to run as fast as she could. She ran past chickens and dogs and children and cows.

In the middle of the village was a pump sticking out of a well. "Water!" Ashanti shrieked. Clean, bright, sparkling water gushed and splattered from the pump.

Children ran in all directions, scrambling for buckets, pots, and pans. Everyone wanted to taste this fresh water. Ashanti stuck her hands under the pump. She splashed that water on her dusty face, and on her aching feet. It sparkled like rainbows in her eyelashes.

Right there, with the children, Ashanti danced on the wet ground. I will never again have to walk a long way carrying a heavy bucket on my head, she thought. And I can go to school! And then I can grow up and be a doctor! All because of the water man.

The water man watched with a smile. Then he asked the villagers if he could explain why he came to their village. The chief gave him permission to speak. The water man told the people that he had wanted to help them but didn't know how, so he asked his God for direction. His God told him to bring water to the people of Tanzania. The water man told the villagers that his God loved them very much, and did not want to see them getting sick from drinking dirty water.

The water man asked if anyone would like to meet this God. Hands shot into the air. Ashanti's mamma's hand and her father's hand shot up. So did Ashanti's hand, still clean and wet. Ashanti was one of the many children and adults who met the wonderful Jesus that day.

Meet The Water For Africa Team

Phil and Julie Hepworth are the founders of Water for Africa, an Australian and Christian not-for-profit organisation. Their mission is to end the statistic that *"One child dies every 90 seconds from a water-related disease"* in Tanzania. This is achieved by showing the love of Christ through the practical means of meeting the Tanzanians' desperate need for clean drinking water and proper sanitation.

Water for Africa work extremely hard to build truly sustainable water projects that are held to a high, measurable standard of success over the long term. Their vision is to see lives changed, and therefore, their focus is not on an ever-growing tally of projects, but on people. Completing the installation of a pump is not the end of a project—it is actually only the beginning.

All proceeds from this book supports Water for Africa's mission. If you wish to support the organisation, please contact them here:

Email: info@waterforafrica.com.au

Website: www.waterforafrica.com.au

Meet The Author

As a mother to a tween and a toddler, Natalie McNee gets the best of both tantrum worlds. Her only escape is to turn the crazy stories and dialogues in her head into exciting children's books. She is married to a burly bouncer, so you don't want to mess with her. Okay, he's really a big teddy bear but don't tell anyone or you'll blow his cover! In addition to *WATER FOR AFRICA*, Natalie is the author of *WHERE ARE SHAYLA'S SOCKS? (Porch Time Publishing, 2018)*, and *NATASHA ROSE MYSTERIES (Dynamo Publishers, 2018)*. Natalie and her husband operate BooksThatBless.Com which publishes testimonials, poetry and books of encouragement. Visit her online at NatalieMcneeBooks.Com, or on Facebook @/NatalieMcNeeBooks and on Instagram @ NatalieMcneeBooks.

Endorsements

Wishes do come true! Children can understand this sentiment and in this book they learn about a wish that they could not imagine needing to wish for. The wish and need for clean water. What a lovely way to share a difficult but real issue with children and show them a true answer to the need.

- David L. Meyer
  CEO of Hand of Hope
  Hand of Hope / Joyce Meyer Ministry

Water for Africa is a beautifully written, delightfully illustrated story about a little girl who dares to dream, and then sees her dream become reality through the provision of water to her village. Full of beauty, hope, and the perspective of a child, it will stir you to want to make a difference in our world.

- Sally Doery
  Senior Pastor, Bridge Church
  Melbourne

Clean water is something that we take for granted in the West. The lack of it in many parts of the world causes disease and death, and means that girls and women, particularly, are trapped into becoming water carriers, bearing this burden for their whole community. The provision of easy-to-access, clean water is one of the greatest, immediate benefits any community can have, and, as Natalie's story tells, has huge knock-on effects in the lives of many girls. What a great project, and what a lovely story by Natalie McNee.

- Cecily Anne Paterson
  Author, writer, speaker

Printed in Great Britain
by Amazon